Rose Plays Hide and Seek

Based on the Original Flower Fairies™ Books
by Cicely Mary Barker

Frederick Warne

One beautiful summer's day, Rose calls
to all her fairy friends.
"Come and play hide-and-seek
with me!"

"What a lovely idea!" says Strawberry. "I've got a special prize for the winner. It's red and sweet and delicious! Can you guess what it is?"

Fairy friends soon flutter around to play the game.

"Buzzzz!" says Bumble Bee from a
nearby flower. "Can I join in?
I'm very good at hiding."

"Of course," laughs Rose.
"We'll all try to find you,
then it'll be someone
else's turn to hide!"

The fairies shut their eyes and start to count.
"One, two, three…" Bumble Bee buzzes off.

"No peeping!" he reminds the fairies.

"...forty-five,
forty-six, forty-seven..."

Nightshade feels something soft brush past his cheek, but he remembers to keep his eyes shut.

He counts out loud to help the little fairies who can't count such big numbers yet.

"...ninety-nine, one hundred!
Ready or not! Here we come!"

The fairies fly off to find their friend Bumble
Bee. They look everywhere! But Bumble Bee
just can't be found.

"Have you seen our friend?"
Michaelmas Daisy asks a passing butterfly.

"Here he is! I've won, I've won!" calls an
excited fairy, pointing to a pretty plant.

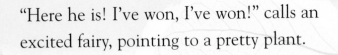

But Beech Tree
smiles and
shakes his
head. "That's
not a bee. It's a flower that
looks like a bee! Keep
looking, everyone!"

The fairies look everywhere, but no one can find Bumble Bee.

Then Scilla has a clever idea. "If we can't find him with our eyes, we'll use our ears!" he says. "Let's just be quiet and listen. Bumble Bee always buzzes when he's happy!"

Sure enough, there's a buzzing sound coming from a nearby flower.

"Found you!" laughs Snapdragon, spotting the busy bee.

"Snapdragon is the winner," cries Strawberry,
"but I think everyone deserves a prize. Come
and help yourselves!"

The fairies and Bumble Bee enjoy a delicious picnic of strawberries and honey in acorn cups.

"Mmmm! Hiding is fun, but finding is even better!" laughs little Rose.

FREDERICK WARNE
Published by the Penguin Group
Penguin Books Ltd, 80 Strand, London WC2R 0RL,
England New York, Australia, Canada, India, New Zealand,
South Africa

This edition first published by Frederick Warne in 2006

1 3 5 7 9 10 8 6 4 2

ISBN 0 7232 5379 X

Printed in China